TM

Based on the Cubix television series,
created by 4Kids Productions

# Botties' Day Off

by Tracey West

## SCHOLASTIC INC.

New York   Toronto   London   Auckland   Sydney
Mexico City   New Delhi   Hong Kong   Buenos Aires

© 2002 CINEPIX, Daiwon, and 4Kids Entertainment. 4Kids Entertainment/ Cubix is a registered trademark of CINEPIX, Daiwon, and 4Kids Entertainment.

ISBN 0-439-40795-8

12 11 10 9 8 7 6 5 4 3 2 1                              2 3 4 5 6 7/0

Designed by Keirsten Geise
Printed in the U.S.A.
First Scholastic printing, October 2002

One sunny day, Connor and Cubix went to the Botties Pit.
"Time to go to work," Connor said.

Abby, Mong, and Chip were ready to work, too.

But Hela had another idea.

"No work today," said Hela. "Go have some fun!"

"You mean we have a day off?" Connor asked.

"HAVE SOME FUN!" said Cubix.

"We can go to the park," said Abby.
"We can have a picnic," said Mong.
They all thought that was a great idea.

The Botties went to the park. They set up their picnic.

"We work hard at the Botties Pit," said Connor. "It is nice to have a day off."

"Let's eat!" said Mong.
But before the Botties could
take a bite, they heard a shout.

"Help! Help!" a man shouted.

"My Hop2ix was hopping," said the man. "It hopped too high. Now it's stuck in this tree!"

"Don't worry," said Connor.
"Cubix can help."

"Cubix, Helicopter!" Connor said.
In a flash, Cubix transformed into
a helicopter.

Cubix and Connor flew up the tall tree.
They saved Hop2ix.
   "Thank you!" said the man.

The Botties went back to their picnic.
"Let's eat!" said Chip.

But the Botties heard another shout.
"Help! Help!" shouted a boy.

"My Amphibix has lost power," said the boy. "Now we're stuck in the lake."

"Don't worry," said Connor.
"Cubix can help."

"Cubix, Jet Ski!" said Connor.
In a flash, Cubix transformed into a Jet Ski.

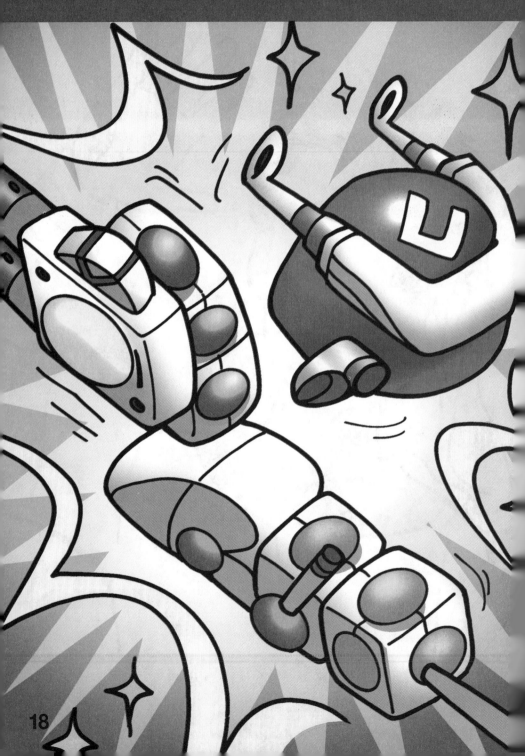

Connor and Cubix zoomed into
the pond. Connor fixed Amphibix.
"Thank you," said the boy.

The Botties went back to their picnic. "Now let's eat!" Abby said.

But the Botties heard another shout.
"Help! Help!" shouted a girl.

"My Mixmutt fell into a deep hole," said the girl. "How will he get out?"

"Don't worry," said Connor. "Cubix will help."

"Cubix, Drill!" said Connor.
In a flash, Cubix transformed into a drill.

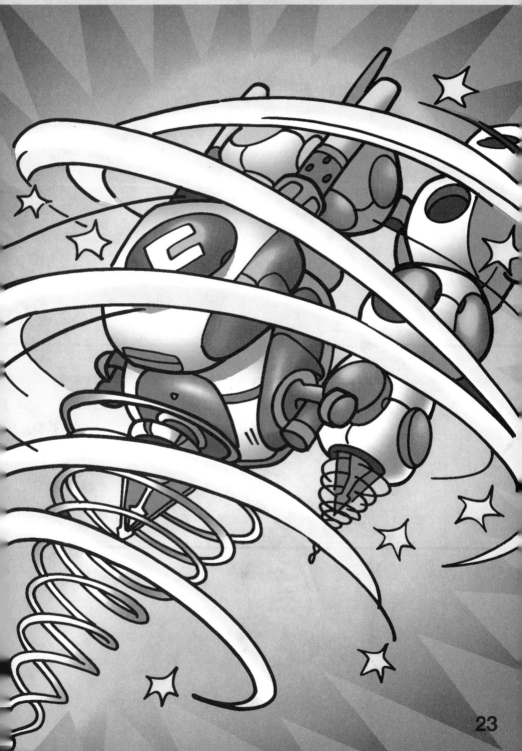

Cubix drilled deep into the ground.
He saved Mixmutt.
"Thank you!" said the girl.

Before the Botties could go back to their picnic, they heard another shout. "Help! Help!" shouted a woman.

"That Disposix is out of control," said the woman. "He's speeding down the hill!"

"Don't worry," said Connor. "Cubix will help."

27

"Cubix, Sports Bike!" Connor said.
In a flash, Cubix transformed into a
sports bike.

Cubix and Connor raced down the hill.
They saved Disposix.
   "Thank you!" said the woman.

"We'll never have our picnic," Mong said.
"This day off is hard work," said Abby.

Connor knew Abby was right. The Botties weren't having much fun at the park.

"Don't worry," Connor said. "I have an idea."

"Can we have our picnic at the Botties Pit?" Connor asked Hela.

"Of course," Hela said. "Just make sure you have fun!"

"HAVE FUN!" said Cubix.